Published by
Princeton Architectural Press
202 Warren Street
Hudson, New York 12534
www.papress.com

Translation rights arranged through the VeroK Agency, Barcelona, Spain

English edition © 2020 Princeton Architectural Press
Printed and bound in China by C&C Offset Printing
23 22 21 20 4 3 2 1 First edition

ISBN 978-1-61689-840-3

This book was illustrated using colored pencil and watercolors.

For Princeton Architectural Press:

Editor: Parker Menzimer
Typesetting: Paula Baver

Special thanks to: Janet Behning, Abby Bussel, Jan Cigliano Hartman,
Susan Hershberg, Kristen Hewitt, Stephanie Holstein, Lia Hunt,
Valerie Kamen, Jennifer Lippert, Sara McKay, Wes Seeley, Rob Shaeffer,
Sara Stemen, Jessica Tackett, Marisa Tesoro, Paul Wagner, and Joseph Weston
of Princeton Architectural Press
—Kevin C. Lippert, publisher

Library of Congress Cataloging-in-Publication Data available upon request.

Little Cheetah's Shadow

Princeton Architectural Press · New York

Little Cheetah had lost something.

"Hello, Little Cheetah," said Bea the firefly.
"What are you looking for?"

"I've lost my shadow," replied Little Cheetah.
"Have you seen it?"

"Why yes! He's sitting above you in the tree," said Bea,
drifting past. "Thanks!" said Little Cheetah.

Little Cheetah climbed into the tree to join
Little Shadow.

Little Shadow looked sad.
"Why did you run away?"
asked Little Cheetah.

"You always get to go first."

"You always get to
choose where we go."

"And you always catch my tail in the door,"
complained Little Shadow.

"Oh! That doesn't sound very nice at all,"
said Little Cheetah.

"From now on, you go first."

Little Shadow was very happy to go first.
And Little Cheetah was happy to stroll behind.
It was a beautiful day.

"Can we stop at Mr. Boubou's bakery?"
asked Little Cheetah.
"I'd like to buy some bread for lunch."

Little Shadow happily agreed.

As they left the bakery, Little Shadow let
the door close on Little Cheetah's tail.

"Ouch!" cried Little Cheetah.
"Oh! Excuse me!" exclaimed Little Shadow.

Little Shadow hadn't done it on purpose.

"That hurt a lot," said Little Cheetah, who now understood why Little Shadow had been upset.

"I didn't even think about it!" said Little Shadow, who now understood why Little Cheetah might not have noticed either.

Little Cheetah and Little Shadow decided that
the best solution might be to walk next to each other.

"Good idea!"

They were almost home, but Little Shadow stopped
at the entrance to a tunnel along the way.

"Oh no!" he cried. "In the dark, I disappear!"

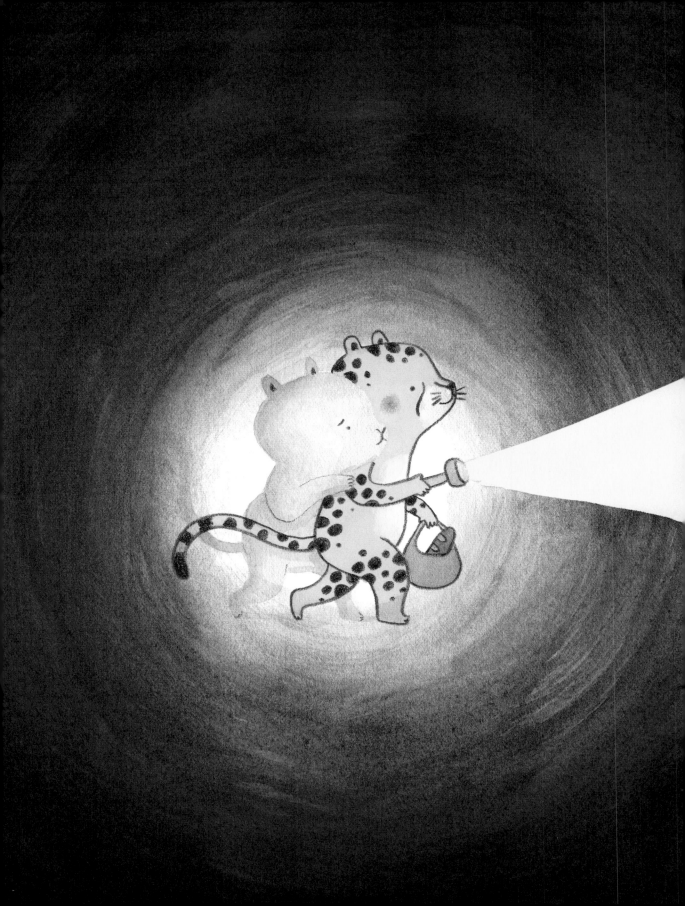

So Little Cheetah
went first
and turned
on his flashlight.

"Stay close to me.
Don't let go," he said.

Little Shadow closed his
eyes and held on
to Little Cheetah.
And together,
they faced the dark.

Happily, home was on
the other side.

"Come in," said Little Cheetah,
holding the door for Little Shadow.

When it was time for bed, Little Cheetah made sure
a night-light was turned on for Little Shadow.

"Good night, Little Shadow."
"Sleep tight, Little Cheetah."